The Magical Animal Fairies

TO Erin,

love Lisa x

D1040404

For Erin and Megan Hale,
with lots of love and
fairy magic

Special thanks to
Sue Mongredien

ORCHARD BOOKS
338 Euston Road, London NW1 3BH
Orchard Books Australia
Level 17/207 Kent Street, Sydney, NSW 2000
A Paperback Original

First published in 2009 by Orchard Books.

© 2009 Rainbow Magic Limited.
A HIT Entertainment company. Rainbow Magic
is a trademark of Rainbow Magic Limited.
Reg. U.S. Pat. & Tm. Off. And other countries.

HiT entertainment

Illustrations © Orchard Books 2009

A CIP catalogue record for this book is available
from the British Library.

ISBN 978 1 40830 351 1
3 5 7 9 10 8 6 4 2

Printed in Great Britain

Orchard Books is a division of Hachette Children's Books,
an Hachette UK company

www.hachette.co.uk

Erin
the Firebird Fairy

by Daisy Meadows

ORCHARD BOOKS

www.rainbowmagic.co.uk

The Fairyland Palace

Barn

Farmhouse

Stables

Clubhouse

CAMP

Adventure Lake

Birdwatching Tower

Jack Frost's
Ice Castle

Meadows

Amphitheatre

The Labyrinth

Cabins

Maze of tunnels

Waterfall

Hills

There are seven special animals
Who live in Fairyland.
They use their magic powers
To help others where they can.

A dragon, black cat, firebird,
A seahorse and snow swan too,
A unicorn and ice bear -
I know just what to do.

I'll lock them in my castle
And never let them out.
The world will turn more miserable,
Of that, I have no doubt...

Contents

Ha Ha!   9

Follow that Firebird!   19

A Close Call   29

Caught in the Net!   41

Joking Aside   53

Go, Go, Giggles   63

Ha Ha!

Kirsty Tate held her breath, trying to keep her fingers steady on the camera as a little brown sparrow only a few steps away pecked at something on the ground. She was crouched at the edge of a woodland clearing, framed by leafy trees and bushes, with dappled sunlight streaming through. She pressed the button on top of the camera. Click! There – perfect.

"Brilliant," said her best friend, Rachel Walker, crouching next to Kirsty. She took her pencil and ticked off the sparrow's picture from a list she held on a clipboard. "That makes five birds we've found and photographed," she said, feeling pleased. "The sparrow, thrush, blackbird, robin and magpie. Just the blue tit to spot now, and we're done."

The two girls were spending a week of their spring holiday at an outdoors adventure camp. Today was Nature Day, and all the campers had been put in pairs and given a list of plants, animals or insects to track down and

photograph. At the end of the day,
they were going to gather around the
campfire and share their discoveries
with everyone.

Rachel and Kirsty sat on a fallen log
to look at the birdwatcher's guidebook
they had been given. Rachel flicked
through until she found a page about
the blue tit. "Here we are," she said,
looking at the photograph. "So it's got
a blue head, wings and tail, and a yellow
chest. Well, that should be easy enough
to spot."

"It says here that the blue tit is
acrobatic and cheeky, and has a funny
call: *tee, tee, tee,*" Kirsty said, reading
aloud. She put her head on one side,
listening hard. "I can't hear anything like
that," she said after a moment.

"I'll have a look with these," Rachel said, picking up their binoculars and scanning the glade. She moved them around slowly, spotting clumps of primroses and nodding daffodils, but no blue tits. The only bird she could see was a robin perched on a tree stump. Rachel chuckled to herself as a joke suddenly popped into her head.

"What's so funny?" Kirsty wanted to know.

"I just thought of a joke," Rachel said. "Which bird steals from the rich to give to the poor?"

"I don't know," Kirsty replied.

"Robin Hood!" Rachel giggled.

Kirsty smiled. "I like that," she said. "I've got one too. Which bird tells the best jokes?"

Rachel shrugged. "I give in," she answered.

"A comedi-HEN!" Kirsty replied.

Both girls laughed.

"My turn," Rachel said. "Why does a hummingbird hum?"

"I don't know," Kirsty said.

"Because it's forgotten the words of the song!" Rachel cried, bursting out laughing. Kirsty too, was helpless with laughter for a few minutes.

Kirsty recovered herself after a while and wiped her eyes. Then she caught sight of something unusual up in the tree tops. "Hey – what's orange, red and yellow and perches on a branch?"

"I don't know," giggled Rachel, thinking it was another joke. "What *is* orange, red and yellow and perches on a branch?"

"No, no," Kirsty said. "I mean it. There's a bird up there, and it's the most beautiful creature I've ever seen. Look!"

Rachel stared up with her binoculars. She blinked in surprise as the bird came into view. It was as big as a parrot, with a long, trailing plume of orange, red and yellow feathers that shone brightly in the sunlight, almost like fire. "Wow," she breathed. "What *is* it?"

Kirsty began leafing through the guidebook to see if she could find a picture that matched the unusual bird, but its pages included nothing remotely like it.

Then the girls were startled by a sudden peal of laughter. It didn't seem quite human, somehow. "What was that?" Kirsty whispered, staring around.

The laughter came again – and Rachel aimed her binoculars at the strange bird. To her amazement, it was tipping its head back, with its beak open, making the laughing sounds! "It…it's the bird!" she said, nudging Kirsty. "The *bird* is laughing. It must be magic!"

Kirsty's mouth fell open in delight as she realised something. "Yes – you're right," she said, smiling. "I bet it's the magical firebird from Fairyland!"

Follow that Firebird!

Rachel nodded. "Of course," she agreed, feeling a prickle of excitement. "The missing firebird – right here in front of us!"

Nobody else at the holiday camp knew, but Rachel and Kirsty had a secret task to carry out that week – they were helping the fairies track down seven missing Magical Animals! Jack Frost had stolen the animals, but they had all escaped from his Ice Castle and found their way into the human world.

The Magical Animals were important to the fairies, because they helped spread some very special qualities around – qualities such as imagination, luck, humour and friendship. Since the animals were only young, though, they weren't quite in control of their powers yet. The Magical Animal Fairies really had to find their charges and take them safely back to Fairyland, before they caused any trouble…but this hadn't been easy so far. Jack Frost had sent out his goblin servants to track down the Magical Animals too, because he didn't want humans or fairies to enjoy their unique gifts. Instead, he wanted everyone to be as miserable as he was!

"I've just realised," Rachel said, as they gazed up at the extraordinary creature. "The firebird's magical gift is humour, isn't it? That's why we've been telling jokes and laughing so much. Just being near the bird is doubling our sense of humour!"

"Oh yes," Kirsty said. "I bet you're right. Well, we need to catch him and return him to Fairyland before any goblins turn up and spot him. Then the joke will definitely be on them!"

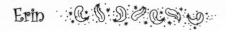

"Let's think of a plan,"
Rachel said – but just as
she spoke, the firebird
took off in a glorious
flash of colour.
It was a
breathtaking
sight! The
creature
flapped its
striking wings,
and the fiery
shades shimmered in the sunshine.

"Quick, let's follow him," Kirsty said,
jumping to her feet and running through
the trees.

Luckily, the firebird's extraordinary
feathers made him easy to see, but he
was fast, and the girls had to race along

22

to keep up. Running whilst gazing up
at the sky was tricky – Rachel almost
tripped over some long tree roots that
were sticking out of the ground.

After a few minutes, the bird landed
on a rock at the other side of a shallow
stream. He folded his wings around
himself, staring about with bright beady
eyes. The girls didn't dare
get too close in case they
scared him away, so they
sat down on the grassy
bank of the stream and
talked in quiet voices.

"Maybe we could lure him across here with some food," Kirsty said thoughtfully. "But what do firebirds like to eat, I wonder?"

"Firecrackers," Rachel joked.

Kirsty smiled too, but then shook her head. "No – we must be serious. We'll never think of a plan if we keep making each other laugh."

Rachel nodded. "Yes, you're right," she said. "Maybe…" Then she broke off as she felt a strange tingling sensation in her jeans pocket, where she had stuffed the birdwatchers' guidebook. She pulled it out quickly…and saw that a page in the middle was glowing with a golden light. This definitely looked like fairy magic!

Her heart thumping, she flipped quickly to the glowing page and opened

the book, holding it out so that both she
and Kirsty could see. It showed a picture
of a very pretty fairy with wavy auburn
hair. She wore an orange-red dress and
sandals, and had a flower tucked in her
hair.

"*Fun Facts about Erin the Firebird
Fairy*," Rachel read aloud.

Kirsty huddled closer to read. "Oh wow," she said, laughing as she saw the list of facts about Erin:

1. She likes making people laugh.

2. She doesn't like it when Jack Frost and his goblins steal things from Fairyland.

3. Her favourite thing in the world is training firebirds to help spread humour throughout both the human and fairy worlds!

"Oh, look, there's a joke," Rachel said, pointing to the bottom of the page. "Knock, knock."

"Who's there?" asked Kirsty.

"Fairy," said Rachel.

"Fairy who?" asked Kirsty.

Rachel was just about to say that the punchline didn't seem to be printed, when they both heard a tinkling laugh. Then a tiny voice finished the joke:

"Fairy pleased to meet you!"

A jet of sparkles poured from the page…and Erin appeared right in front of their eyes!

A Close Call

Erin fluttered her sparkly wings, grinning. "Hello!" she said in her silvery voice. "How lovely to see you again. Tell me, do you know what gets bigger the more you take away from it?"

"I don't know," Rachel replied with a smile. "What *does* get bigger the more you take away from it?"

"A hole!" Erin replied, clapping her hands together.

Kirsty and
Rachel didn't
laugh.
They both
understood
the joke, but for
some reason, they
didn't find it very funny.

Erin's smile turned to a frown. "Ahh,"
she said. "I think Giggles the firebird
must be nearby, you know. He's very
clever, but hasn't quite finished his
training. Sometimes, he zaps the humour
out of a joke instead of zinging it *in*."

"Giggles *is* nearby," Kirsty told her.
"Look – he's just over there on the rock."
She pointed to where the firebird was
perched behind the fairy's back, and Erin
spun round immediately.

A broad grin crossed her face and she opened her mouth to call to him. But just then two boys from the camp rushed out from the undergrowth. Erin had to dart quickly out of sight behind a bush, and Giggles flew away at the noise, high up into the tree tops.

"Hi Tommy, hi Jason," Kirsty said, recognising the boys. "What are you up to?"

"We've been given a list of butterflies to find," dark-haired Tommy replied, holding up a clipboard and guidebook. "We were hiding behind the bushes there, and spotted a golden butterfly fluttering around you two."

"We think it's a clouded yellow, which is the last one on our list," Jason added, pushing his glasses up his nose as he spoke. "Did you see which way it went?"

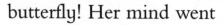

Uh-oh. Rachel felt alarmed as she realised that the boys must have seen *Erin*, and mistaken her for a butterfly! Her mind went blank with panic. What should she say to throw the boys off the scent? "Um…" she began, thinking wildly. Then she realised that she could actually tell the truth.

"I haven't seen a butterfly all day," she replied honestly.

"We've been too busy birdwatching."

"Bird *chasing*, more like," Kirsty added.

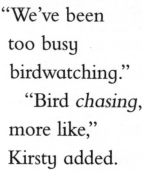

The boys fell about laughing, clutching at each other helplessly. Jason almost dropped his camera, he was laughing so hard!

Rachel and Kirsty exchanged surprised glances. Kirsty's comment hadn't been *that* funny! "Giggles must be at it again," Rachel whispered to Kirsty. "But this time he's zapped too much humour into a joke!"

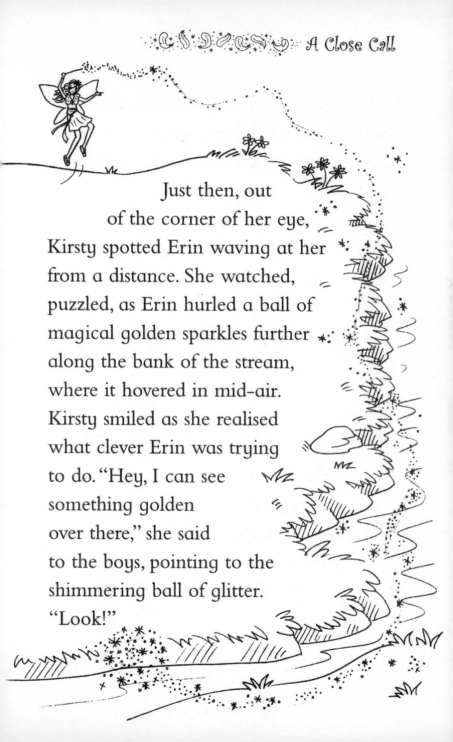

Just then, out
of the corner of her eye,
Kirsty spotted Erin waving at her
from a distance. She watched,
puzzled, as Erin hurled a ball of
magical golden sparkles further
along the bank of the stream,
where it hovered in mid-air.
Kirsty smiled as she realised
what clever Erin was trying
to do. "Hey, I can see
something golden
over there," she said
to the boys, pointing to the
shimmering ball of glitter.
"Look!"

The boys stopped laughing and turned to follow where Kirsty was pointing. Erin seemed to be working some magic that was making the ball move along so that, from a distance, it did look rather like a butterfly. "Cool! Thanks, Kirsty," Tommy said. "Come on, Jason, let's go!"

The boys raced off towards the magical golden sparkles, and Erin fluttered out from her hiding place.

"Phew," she said. "That was a close one. Humans must *never* find out about us fairies, or our Fairyland home."

"Apart from us," Rachel added.

Erin smiled. "Yes, apart from you two, of course. But you help us all the time and we trust you. Other humans might not be as friendly."

The fairy gazed up to where Giggles had been perched in one of the trees. "Oh," she said in dismay. "Giggles has flown away! I didn't see him go – did either of you two?"

Kirsty shook her head. "No," she said. "I didn't dare look up at him while the boys were with us, in case they wondered what I was doing." She stared around hopefully at all the tree tops, but there was no sign of the firebird's fiery feathers. "Oh, no," she groaned. "Where could he be? We've got to find him again – and quickly!"

Caught in the Net!

The three friends set out along the
edge of the stream in search of Giggles.
Rachel and Kirsty took turns with their
binoculars, while Erin took out her own
pair of tiny fairy binoculars to peer
through.

"Wow, look," Rachel said, after they'd been walking for a few minutes. "There are some other birdwatchers over there, up in the tower. They're all dressed up and everything!"

She passed the binoculars to Kirsty so she could see. The tower was built of wood and was as tall as the oak trees surrounding it. At the top of the tower was a viewing platform, where four birdwatchers stood. They were all dressed in camouflage-patterned clothes so that they blended into the trees. The birdwatchers also wore wide-brimmed green hats and each

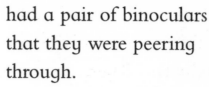

had a pair of binoculars
that they were peering
through.

"Wow, they're taking it
very seriously," Kirsty
commented. "They've even
painted their faces green too,
so that they match the
leaves." She looked up
at them again and
noticed that one of
the birdwatchers
was now jumping
up and down
excitedly, pointing
at something
upstream. His
friends all turned
and looked – and

then *they* began to jump up and down too! Then, as one of them jumped extra high, his hat fell off, and Kirsty gasped as she got a proper look at his face.

"Rachel, Erin!" she hissed, as she saw what a long green nose the hatless birdwatcher had. "They aren't birdwatchers with painted faces – they're goblins!"

Erin let out a little squeak of alarm. "And why are they so excited?" she wondered, turning her binoculars in the direction the goblins had been pointing.

Then she took a sharp intake of breath.

"Oh – I know why!" she exclaimed. "They've seen Giggles – he's perched on a log about twenty metres past the viewing tower!"

"We've got to get to him first," Rachel said at once. "Look – that goblin is carrying a net. We just can't let them catch poor Giggles!"

"Come on," Kirsty said, and she and Rachel began running along the stream, with Erin flying above their heads. The goblins, meanwhile, were all pushing and shoving each other in their haste to get down the steps of the wooden tower.

As the girls came nearer, the goblins pelted down the last few steps and shot off ahead, one with a net clasped in his hand.

"We won't be able to catch up with them on foot," Rachel panted. "Erin, can you turn us into fairies? We'll be able to go much faster if we can fly."

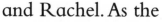

"Of course," Erin replied and quickly waved her wand over the girls. A stream of orange fairy dust floated out from her wand's tip and swirled all around Kirsty and Rachel. As the magic sparkles touched them, the girls felt themselves shrinking smaller and smaller...until they were the same size as Erin. Now they each had a pair of gauzy wings, and with a few quick flutters, Rachel and Kirsty had zoomed up into the air to join their friend.

"After them!" cried Kirsty excitedly,

flapping her wings as hard as she could. She, Erin and Rachel all zoomed through the air, taking care to fly high so that the goblins wouldn't notice them.

It's very difficult flying so quickly through the trees! Rachel thought, swerving past a pine tree and taking care not to snag her wings on its dark green needles. It was like a fairy obstacle course, zipping over and under branches, dodging the tree trunks and having to dive out of the way of the birds and butterflies that were flying through the wood.

Down below, the goblins were all running along at great speed – and there, further ahead, was Giggles, sitting on the log and preening his long tail feathers.

"Watch out, Rachel!" Erin suddenly called, and Rachel jerked her attention back to where she was going – to see that a song-thrush was headed straight for her!

With a cry of alarm, Rachel just managed to swerve out of the way at the last second, and the thrush passed safely by. Rachel's wings trembled with shock at the near-miss. If the thrush's sharp beak had accidentally caught one of her wings, it would have been a disaster!

"Are you all right?" Kirsty called over, risking a glance across at her friend.

Rachel nodded, concentrating so hard on where she was flying, she didn't dare speak.

"We're nearly there," Erin said. "Giggles is just below us. Oh no!"

Kirsty and Rachel glanced down, wondering why Erin had cried out… just in time to see one of the goblins throwing his net over Giggles. The firebird was trapped!

Joking Aside

Rachel felt dismayed. This was awful news! "Gotcha!" she heard one of the mean goblins cheering from below and felt sick at the thought of beautiful Giggles being caught by one of them.

"We need a plan," Kirsty said, flying to perch on a nearby branch and gesturing to the others to follow her. "At least the goblins don't know we're here. If we're quick, we can think of some way to trick them and get Giggles back."

The three fairies peered down at the goblins, who were all congratulating each other on a job well done.

"Brilliant work, mate," one of them said to the goblin with the net, slapping him on the back. "You were so quick – and so sneaky!"

The goblins were doing high-fives and looking really pleased with themselves. "Jack Frost is going to be so happy," one said. "He might even smile – imagine that!"

The mention of smiling reminded Rachel of earlier, when she and Kirsty had been smiling and giggling at jokes. Then she remembered how they'd been absolutely helpless with laughter at one point…and an idea popped into her head.

"I've got it," she said to Erin and Kirsty, her eyes shining.

"What if we can make the goblins laugh
– *really* laugh, I mean, like we were
laughing, Kirsty? With Giggles nearby to
strengthen their humour, we can tell them
some jokes and hopefully they'll all be
rolling about in no time. And then, with
a bit of luck, we'll be able to rescue
Giggles from the net."

"I love it!" Kirsty exclaimed. "Great
idea, Rachel!"

Erin didn't look quite so sure. "It's a
good idea, but we'll have to hope that
Giggles' magic is
working properly," she
said. "You saw what
happened earlier,
when he zapped the
humour out of my
joke – it killed it stone

dead, and you two didn't even smile! If the same thing happens again, any joke you tell the goblins will fall flat, and they won't laugh. Even worse, it'll make them really suspicious of you."

"I see what you mean," Rachel said, "but I still think we should try. I can't think of any other ideas to help Giggles escape – can you two?"

Kirsty shook her head.

"It's definitely worth a try," Erin said. "Let's fly down lower, behind those bushes, and I'll turn you back into girls.

Then I'll just have to cross my fingers
and hope that Giggles can pull it off!"

The three fairies fluttered down
behind some brambles where the goblins
wouldn't be able to see them, and Erin
waved her wand again at Kirsty and
Rachel, chanting some magic words as
she did so. With another swirl of fairy
dust, Kirsty and Rachel felt
their wings vanish
as they grew
back to their
normal size.

The two girls
came out from
behind the
brambles and
approached
the goblins.

The goblins didn't look at all pleased to see them – and one of them held up a warning hand. "Stop there," he said. "Keep your distance. We've got the firebird and there's nothing you can do about it now."

Rachel shrugged as if she wasn't really interested. "Oh, right," she said coolly. "We just came over to tell you a funny joke, actually. We thought you might like a laugh after all your hard work." She could see the goblins were about to disagree, so she ploughed straight on with it. "What does Jack Frost like to eat for breakfast?"

The goblins looked at each other and shrugged. "Don't know," one replied.

"Frosties!" Rachel cried, grinning.

Kirsty watched the goblins' faces eagerly, hoping they would find Rachel's joke funny. Unfortunately, though, they didn't even smile.

"I don't get it," one of the goblins muttered, looking confused.

"Jack Frost doesn't even eat breakfast," another said scornfully.

Kirsty and Rachel exchanged worried glances. Oh dear. Giggles' magic wasn't working very well at all. They had to make the goblins fall about laughing if they were to stand a chance of rescuing the firebird – but at this rate, that was never going to happen!

Go, Go, Giggles

Kirsty tried next. "How about this one: what do you get if you cross Jack Frost with a vampire?" she asked. "Frost bite!"

This time, the goblins smiled. One of them even chuckled. "Frost bite, I like that," he said.

Feeling encouraged, Rachel gave them another one. "How does Jack Frost travel to work?" she asked. "By icicle!"

Yes! The goblins all burst out laughing. "Not bicycle – icicle!" one of them chortled, shaking with laughter.

Kirsty grinned at Rachel. The plan was working! "What did Jack Frost say to Frosty the Snowman?" she asked them. "Have an ice day!"

"Have an ice day!" one of the goblins repeated, clutching his middle and guffawing.

"How do you keep a goblin in suspense?" Rachel asked them next.

"We don't know," the goblins spluttered in reply.

"We'll tell you tomorrow!" Rachel and Kirsty chorused.

At this, the goblins all fell over with laughter. They were rolling around on the ground, shoulders shaking, tears of mirth streaming down their cheeks. "I get it!" one chuckled. "We're goblins and they're keeping us in suspense!"

"Hilarious!" another gasped, thumping the ground as he chortled.

Kirsty and Rachel looked at each other, then at the goblins' net, which was on the ground, with Giggles trapped inside. The goblins were still helpless with laughter.

"Now!" Kirsty hissed.

Without any further hesitation, the girls ran to the net and lifted it up. Erin flew over to them, her arms outstretched. "Giggles! I'm here!" she called.

Giggles blinked, shook out his feathers and then gave a happy laugh as he saw his fairy mistress. He flapped his shimmering wings and flew out of the net and up into the air towards Erin, shrinking down to fairy size as he went.

Giggles looked
so sweet as he
flew into Erin's
arms. He
nestled his head
on her shoulder
and let out peals
of melodic
giggles. "Hello,
sweetie," Erin
said, stroking him
gently. Then she
laughed, too. "Oh, it's so
good to have you back again!"

The goblins, meanwhile, were still
rolling about with laughter, and Giggles
let out an amused chirp as the tears ran
down their green cheeks. "We'd better
leave them to it," Erin said to Kirsty and

Rachel in a low voice. "Once they realise they don't have the firebird any more, they'll have to go back to Fairyland and tell Jack Frost. They won't find that quite so funny, unfortunately."

"Goodbye Erin, goodbye Giggles," Rachel said, patting the little bird's downy feathers. "Thanks for all the laughs."

"Yes, that was the funniest adventure we've had for a long time!" Kirsty smiled. "Goodbye!"

Erin waved and smiled as she and Giggles flew off in a shower of sparkles. Rachel and Kirsty watched until the last magical sparkle had vanished, then turned to one another. "We'd better go back to camp," Kirsty said. "I'm so glad we helped Erin find Giggles – but it's a shame we didn't manage to spot all the birds on our list."

The two girls took a few steps away
from the goblins, and then Rachel froze,
clutching Kirsty's arm. "*Tee, tee, tee!*"
they heard.

Kirsty grinned in delight as she spotted
a small yellow and blue bird on the
branch of a nearby tree. "A blue tit!" she
whispered, fumbling to switch on the
camera. She held it out then pressed the
button… Click!

She and Rachel watched the blue tit
as it hopped along the branch, then
fluttered away. "We did it!" Rachel
cheered, ticking it off on her list.
"Hooray! I can't wait to tell
everyone about the
birds we saw."

Kirsty grinned
and slipped an
arm through
Rachel's as they
headed back
towards camp.
"Me too," she
said. "But we
won't tell them
about *all* the
birds we saw!"

The Magical Animal Fairies

Erin the Firebird Fairy has got her
Magical Animal back! Now Rachel
and Kirsty must help...

Rihanna
the Seahorse Fairy

Adventure Lake

"Oh, I'm really looking forward to going canoeing again!" Kirsty Tate said eagerly to her best friend Rachel Walker. The girls were carrying a lightweight canoe on their shoulders as they walked through the camp towards Adventure Lake. "But I'm going to try to keep my feet dry this time!"

Rachel laughed. "Yes, it's good fun, isn't it?" she agreed. "I'm glad we've got some free time this afternoon so that we can have another go."

"We're not just here to have fun

though, are we?" Kirsty added, glancing around to check that none of the other campers were close enough to hear. "We're trying to help our fairy friends, too!"

On the day the girls arrived at the adventure camp, the King and Queen of Fairyland had asked for their help to find the seven missing Magical Animals. These special young animals had amazing powers that helped to spread the kind of magic that humans as well as fairies could possess – the wonderful gifts of imagination, good luck, humour, friendship, compassion, healing and courage.

The seven Magical Animal Fairies spent a whole year training these magical youngsters before they returned to their families in Fairyland, ready to use their special talents to help everyone in both the human and the fairy worlds. However, spiteful Jack Frost was determined to put a stop to all this, simply because he wanted everyone to be as cold and uncaring as he was himself.

So he and his naughty goblin servants had kidnapped the Magical Animals and taken them to his Ice Castle. But the animals had managed to escape, and now they had hidden themselves away in the human world. Rachel and Kirsty were determined to find all seven Magical Animals before Jack Frost and his goblins did, and then return them safely to Fairyland...

Calling all Rainbow Magic fans
– the fairies need YOUR help!

Wicked Jack Frost has stolen

7 precious, glittering Jewel Fairy wands

and hidden them in 7 secret locations all over the country.

For your chance to WIN one of the 7 magical wands
AND to feature in a Rainbow Magic book
you must solve the clues in our Rainbow Magic Treasure Hunt!

To take part, all you have to do is:

1) Buy a copy of the special £1 Treasure Hunt edition of
Hannah the Happy Ever After Fairy (in shops from July 2009),
which contains a secret code.

2) Log on to **www.rainbowmagic.co.uk**, enter the special code
and select the region nearest to where you live.

3) Download your own special Rainbow Magic Treasure Map
and get your first Treasure Hunt clue telling you how to begin!

The first clue will be on the website on **Friday 3 July 2009**
and the Fun Day Fairies will be revealing a clue
every Friday for 7 weeks until **Friday 14 August 2009**,
when the last clue will be revealed.

Good Luck!

The Magical Animal Fairies

Win Rainbow Magic goodies!

In every book in the Magical Animal Fairies series
(books 71-77) there is a hidden picture of a pawprint with
a secret letter in it. Find all seven letters and re-arrange them to
make a special Magical Animal Fairies word, then send it to us.
Each month we will put the entries into a draw and select one
winner to receive a Rainbow Magic sparkly T-shirt and goody bag!

Send your entry on a postcard to Rainbow Magic Magical Animal
Fairies Competition, Orchard Books, 338 Euston Road, London
NW1 3BH. Australian readers should write to Hachette Children's
Books, Level 17/207 Kent Street, Sydney, NSW 2000.
New Zealand readers should write to Rainbow Magic Competition,
4 Whetu Place, Mairangi Bay, Auckland, NZ. Don't forget to
include your name and address. Only one entry per child.
Final draw: 30th April 2010.

Good luck!

Have you checked out the

website at:
www.rainbowmagic.co.uk

Look out for the

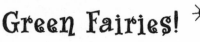 Green Fairies!

NICOLE
THE BEACH FAIRY
978-1-40830-474-7

ISABELLA
THE AIR FAIRY
978-1-40830-475-4

EDIE
THE GARDEN FAIRY
978-1-40830-476-1

CORAL
THE REEF FAIRY
978-1-40830-477-8

LILY
THE RAINFOREST FAIRY
978-1-40830-478-5

CARRIE
THE SNOW CAP FAIRY
978-1-40830-479-2

MILLY
THE RIVER FAIRY
978-1-40830-480-8

Available
September 2009

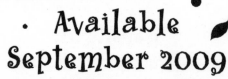